# Can't Catch Me!

## Michael Foreman

Andersen Press
London

"Goodnight, Little Monkey," said Mum.
"Sweet dreams."

"No! It's too early for bed,"
said Little Monkey . . .

"Can't catch ME!"

"RRRROAR!
ARRROOO!
Coming to get you and when we do . . ."

"Can't catch ME!"

"GRRRRRR!

GARRRRRROOO!

Coming to get you and when we do . . ."

"Can't catch ME!"

"HRRRRUMF! HARRRROOO! Coming to get you and when we do . . ."

"WALLUMF, WALLUMF, WALLUMF, WALLOO!

Coming to get you and when we do . . . "

"Can't catch ME!"

"SNAPPETTY SNAP, SNACKAROOO! Coming to get you and when we do . . ."

"Can't Catch ME . . ."

"BEEP BEEP, BEEP BEEP, BEEP BEEP, BOOO!

Coming to get you and when we do . . ."

"Can't catch ME!"

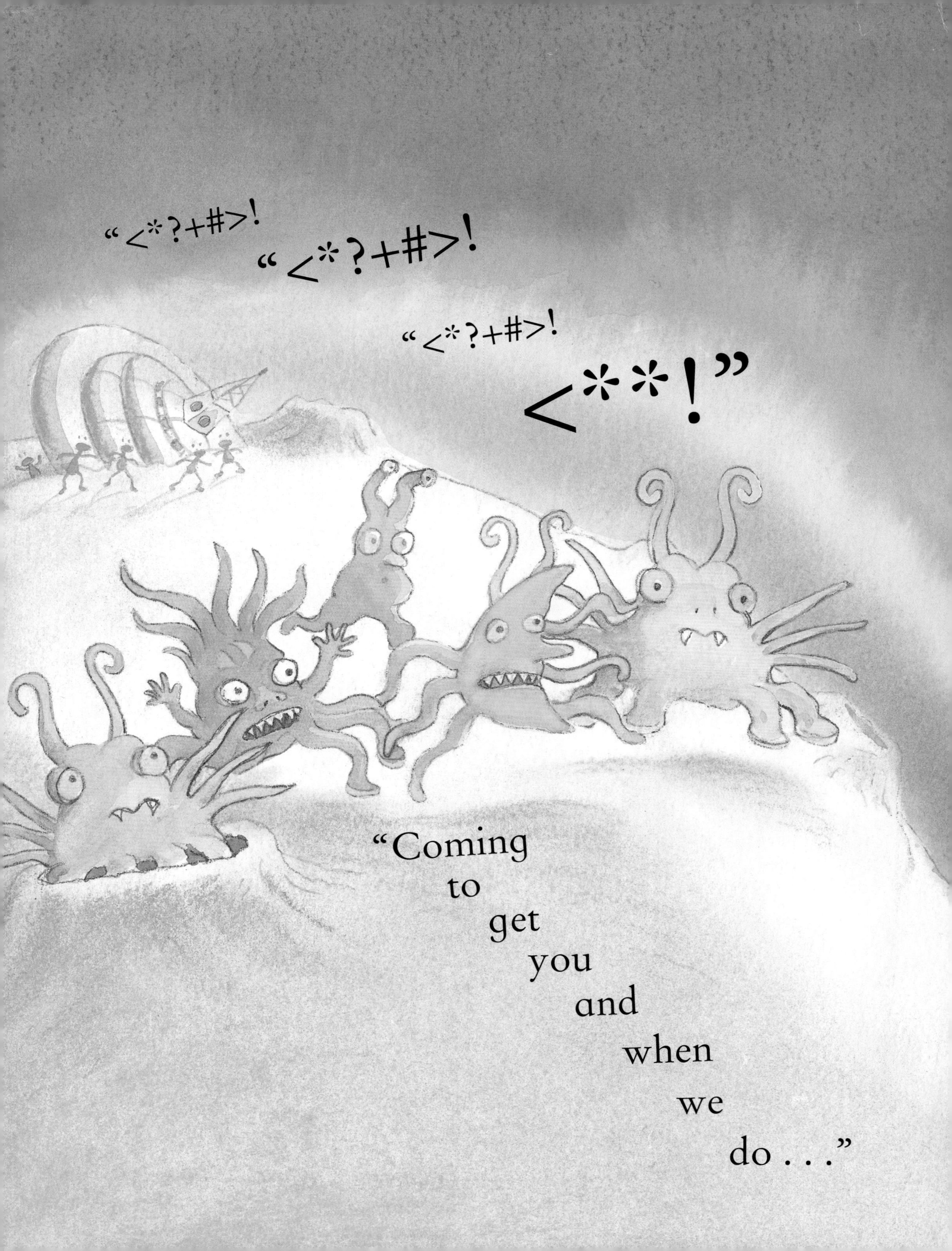

"<*?+#>!

"<*?+#>!

"<*?+#>!

<**!"

"Coming
to
get
you
and
when
we
do . . ."

"Can't catch . . .

. . . Meeeee!"

# "HARRAH! HARROOO!

Now we'll get you —
and we're going to . . .

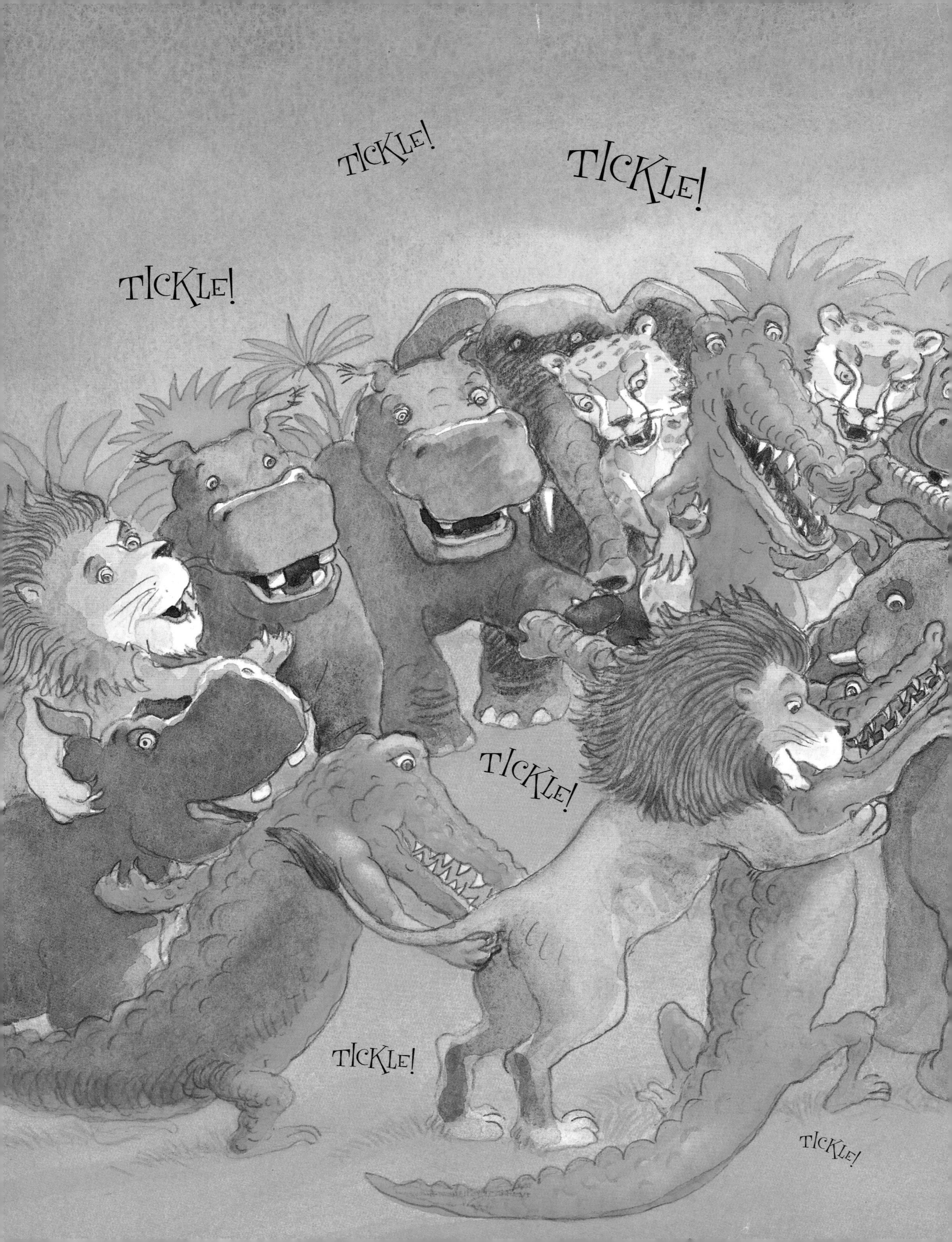

TICKLE!

TICKLE!

TICKLE!

TICKLE!

TICKLE!

TICKLE!

"Hee, hee, hee . . .